A
CERTAIN
SHADE
OF
LIPSTICK

LUKE SETTLE

For the needles in the classroom

PROLOGUE

He had a pokey face.

The kind that looked like it had more bone than skin. The kind that looked like it was caving in on itself. His jawline was prominent and his eyes were beady — beady like the rain that slid down the glass of our bedroom window, especially during that winter's evening.

His eyebrows were almost entwined within his eyelashes, they were almost in unity. His face had the prickly resemblance of desert cacti. Not quite as dry but just as sharp, in multiple ways. His eyes were grey. Piercingly grey. They glinted in every direction but they seemed to glint just that little bit more when they stared back at me. His height stretched out what very little mass he carried. His body was slender and his face was gaunt. His hair was receding but there was enough of it to resemble a style. Splinters of hair that had been flicked back with a comb, stiffened by mousse and hairspray shone reflectively in dim artificial light.

He had a pokey face — the man I watched on my wife … especially during that winter's evening.

1

Have you ever questioned the desires that lie within? Questioned the deeper desires that are kept hidden, out of reach? I know I have and often still delve back in to those depths for answers. My insecurities rival my confidence and propel my malaise. This must have been confusing to most, even ironic in some way. I was secure financially, in companionship and in love but then again security never actually *comforted* me, it simply accompanied me — strapped to me like a backpack full of things I thought were daily necessities. I'm not calling her insane nor have I ever questioned her logic. I'm simply trying to make sense of why her eyes shifted my way that warm summer's evening outside the Alabama Bar in Faliraki. I'm asking why her lips pressed against mine hours later and why we awoke within the same bed at the same time the ocean slid up and spread itself against the rocks within the bay.

Why did she choose me? Does it even matter anymore? We're back to those comforts again and knowing that she did choose me is a fact that gave me some comfort back when it mattered but let's park that bus there and expand on how she became the ray of light that once peered and pierced its way through my heart.

Maria was fifty percent Greek, fifty percent English and a further hundred percent of pure olive beauty. She had flown back to her mother's birthplace in England when her mother had decided to separate from her father who seemingly couldn't separate himself from the bottle. Maria's mother escaped back to North Yorkshire and took with her her only child, introducing Maria to a beauty that only the natives truly appreciated — the English countryside. Maria's mother claimed that the wet and muddy hills had the power to hide anyone from life's wickedness and as they both knew, Maria's father could be extremely wicked. What her mother also knew was something that she had continued to tell herself for years whilst absorbing the abuse from her husband, familiarity is a face that welcomes you home.

Maria's mother fell for the glitter that has surrounded so many other holiday romances. She was blinded enough to eventually marry her Greek god. Once the glitter wore off, the bruises appeared and she spent more and more time recycling glass bottles to avoid being hit by them. Maria was never put off by her mother's stories and never dismissed the possibility that a holiday romance could in fact work. It fuelled her enough to believe that the void left from her father and the emptiness from her own emotional detachment could one day both be filled by one man. She dreamed of the day that she would find somebody to not only love her but to protect her as well. Maria kept her father's culture in her blood and her mother's love in her heart. She returned home to the island of Rhodes every summer but never once went to see her abusive father. She knew he was somewhere on the island, drowning himself in spirits.

In the summer of 2004 when Maria had thirty years of life behind her, she visited Faliraki to hook up with old friends. They chinwagged for hours on end about how different their lives were. Once they were all talked out (which usually took up an entire morning and most of an afternoon) they would head out to a local bar. One thats primary purpose was to entertain the tourists by encouraging them to ruin once-great songs in a drunken state over a cheap microphone. More often than not, the off-key singing was also out of time to the coloured-in lyrics on screen. Maria and her friends went out to the Alabama Bar each and every night of the two weeks that

4

Maria was there for. Sometimes they would stay for an hour, sometimes six. It was run by the same family that had run it when Maria and her friends were growing up, so drinks were free. They returned the favour by directing tourists to the bar which was why it was always rammed. It wasn't just the owners that supplied the drinks though, they'd get drinks and go two's on ciggy's from tourists who mistook their sarcasm for flirting. Genetically, men were deemed to be slow at maturing but on this Greek island they seemed to be slow at just the basics. *A pocket full of cash for a piece of ass* is what Maria was taught by her mother, who had passed down the unfortunate English trait of mimicking whatever slang and catchphrases the Americans were using at that particular time. She was cryptically telling her daughter to at least get *something* for accepting a request to wiggle her tooshie.

Maria was not prepared for '04, she was not prepared for me. She had no idea that her eyes would uncontrollably switch focus from her friends and over to me for the entirety of the night. Her eyes often slowed down as they swept across her friends and travelled en-route back to mine. She was careful enough to not jeopardise the situation. She wouldn't want any of her single and carefree friends to notice that she had begun to home in on someone that may possess the qualities to preoccupy her from coming back to the island each year. Maria was different though. She wasn't entirely like her friends and Yorkshire was responsible for that. She lived in the countryside, not by a tourist leisure resort made for Brits. It changes you and it had changed Maria. Along with her upbringing she knew that she wanted love, she wanted that happily ever after that her mother never got. She would bite her lip when our eye contact became too intense, circling the straw inside her cocktail glass just to divert her attention but the temptation to raise her eyes just one more time often got the better of her. I sat there with my two friends, opposite Maria and hers.

She wasn't interested in free drinks and I wasn't interested in karaoke.

2

The morning after the night before felt like a fantasy. I felt like I had been punched to death. The reality was, I was the one doing the punching — punching way above my weight. I ached from hours of physical exploration and I throbbed from pleasure. I must have blinked a million times to reassure myself that this was indeed not a fantasy. Maria was beautiful. Long dark hair that had a coiled spring inside itself. A natural wavy flick that enticed me to feel young again and embrace the ride like a Scalextric track. Her skin was a light olive shade, even in winter she had colour.

That evening we both made excuses to our friends so that we could leave the bar early. I walked out first and moments later, she followed. We were both adults and we knew where the evening was going. We left the Alabama Bar and teasingly wandered across the beach, kicking small sand dunes along the way. We asked all the basic questions one asks upon meeting a stranger, all the polite crap that won't matter at all once you get to where you want. The closer we got to her apartment the more my brain became fuzzy. I was initially dazzled by her beauty but then her intelligence became evident in conversation. We had talked for a little more than an hour before she decided to whisper something in my ear. A gentle combination of words that rendered me powerless yet somehow gave me strength. Maria weaved herself through my barrier of comfort and slowly whispered, "*Parakaló.*" I had no idea what she was trying to say but each syllable tickled the hairs within my ear to form a symphony that played throughout my body. I was paralysed and my statue-like posture revealed my true weakness to her. "It's ok," she said affectionately, "it'll all make sense." A simple word she spoke to me from between her certain shade of lipstick had tranced and seduced me. I had no idea what it meant and as her apartment came into view, I had to know. "Maria, what did that mean … back there on the beach?"

"*Parakaló?*" She effortlessly teased in her native accent. "Yeah, that?"

"It means … my little English boy … you're welcome." "Huh?" I spat out in the most common British way I could.

"It means, you're welcome. You know, like something you'd say *after* saying thank y—?"

"But I didn't say thank you?" I corrected whilst inter- rupting. Maria smiled, almost patronisingly. "Here!" She shrieked, then pointed upwards as she stumped out the cigarette that we had shared along the way. "This is me!" It actually wasn't, it was her friend's apartment but finer details held no relevance here. I asked no more questions. Tonight wasn't about manners, it wasn't about small talk. It was about luck and seeing the look in her eyes as she wet her lips made me feel like an Irish leprechaun.

3

Every morning after my first night with Maria tasted sweeter. During that evening in '04 we made love for longer than I believed possible, we made love better than I believed possible. As I finished for the last time during our evening together I lay their limp, lifeless and mesmer-

7

ised. She was silent, shaking in the heat. I eventually hovered on top of Maria's smooth, silk-like breasts as I kissed the coves behind her ears. I retreated from her ear coves and gently whispered, "Thank you."

I look back now and believe she saw a future in us from that very first evening. She knew I was going to thank her that night because she was always going to give me a reason to. Maria smiled after I spoke the words that she had predetermined. Laying there underneath me, her silk-like breasts looked glossy in the midnight hour. We held each other's eyes before regarding each other's naked vulnerability further. Before the sun came up, she wet her lips in a way that seemed to slow time before she whispered against the moonlight air, "*Parakaló.*"

4

I wasn't a popular kid at school, not one of the cool kids. I imagine Maria was. I imagine Maria was the wet dream of every teenager's thoughts. As a teenager myself I succumbed to the puppy fat phase and never really out-grew it. Instead my skin outgrew my bones as I was al-ways comforted by the grease that lay within my favourite foods. I had two friends growing up, Jack Toddinger and Clayton Reams. Jack and Clay were much cooler than me, both saw me as their prodigy because I was clever and they were popular. It was an odd mix to the majority but it worked. We never drifted, even well past secondary school. My aspirations to become a games developer paid off at the detriment of a social life. I ended up working for Push my Buttons, a mediocre games developer that separated kids even further from reality. I guess I was partly responsible for turning mummy's little baby into mummy's little monster. I helped provide a platform to demonstrate keyboard warrior skills. Mix this with pro-fanity down headsets and I guess the transformation was complete. As for Jack and Clay, they continued down the only roads they knew. They continued to attend trials for numerous local football teams, occasionally getting minor breaks along the way. The closer we all got to thirty though, the more sour reality began to taste and so both boys had the painful realisation that their time had pretty much ran out. They exchanged their part-time jobs into full-time slave labour receiving only the national minim-um wage. Jack became a chef at the luxurious J D Weth-erspoon and Clayton became a cinema attendant at the local Showcase Cinema. We were all underpaid but we were still in contact and it was at the age of thirty when we decided to have a blow-out and go to Greece for a summer holiday. One last holiday before getting our actu-al shit together, a proper boys holiday. A lads holiday. Jack and Clay were single, players on and off the field. I played with software and squashed digital bugs. A holiday seemed like a great way for me to dust the cobwebs down. That's how we ended up in Faliraki and that's how I met Maria, Maria with that undeniably unique shade of lip-stick.

5

2009 came round fast and although we were in the same country, we were counties apart. She lived in North Yorkshire and I lived in Lincolnshire. We spoke regularly on the phone but it wasn't enough for me. Maria was unwilling to commit to being anything more than a week-end girlfriend due to her mother's illness. She had an ag-gressive and sudden cancer spread throughout the whole of her body. Maria believed the cause of her mother's cancer to be from 'love bruises'. A term Maria used to symbolise the physical wounds her father used to inflict on her. I had been seeing Maria for nearly five years and I wanted to take things further, make us more secure, make her mine. The catalyst to Maria's departure from North Yorkshire (and the answer to my prayers) was her mother's defeat. In the late spring of '09 Maria's mother lost her battle with cancer. I know it's a selfish way to look at it but by the autumn of '09, I guess Maria finally became mine. Her mother's home had become a nook for old memories too painful to bear. We married two years later and although I was nearly touching forty, my wife made every day feel like I was back in '04.

6

"Lights out! Shut up!" The order was barked at volume and followed by the subsequent clunking and clanging of metal. The order and its accompanied metallic backing powered their way into my eardrums where they bounced around in my skull at such velocity I nearly shouted back at the—

7

I plodded along in my job pleasing gaming junkies in their quest for online domination. Jack and Clay struggled, moaning like frustrated zombies living through similar eight hour shifts five days a week. Deep down I knew they envied my life, 'the geek with the Greek' is how they put it to me. Neither had committed themselves to my type of lifestyle and I doubted that they ever would.

Maria never picked up her career again after moving down south. Instead, she worked in a local charity shop that supported cancer. It brought her comfort that in turn brought some internal peace. She was giving back to a world that had taken something so dear from her. She had tipped the scales of morality in her favour and so in her mind, god would now be in her debt! She was still very bitter about her mum and often spat insults to him up above as she dragged eagerly on her pack of twenty Mayfair — I was always a Lambert type of guy. She teased the big man whilst exhaling smoke from her lungs. She directed the cancer clouds skywards as she would say, "See you soon gatekeeper." In contrast she would immediately look down and tease, "Or is it with you where I'll end up?" Both gatekeepers were ready and waiting, they always were.

8

The closer we got to forty, the more Maria began to change. She began to pay particular attention to Jack. Though, it wasn't the fact that she was paying him more attention, it was the fact that her attention seemed to be attracting him.

9

"Psst! Oi. Psst! Are you awake? Hey, Paperboy! Are you a-fucking-wake?" The aggressive whispering bounced off my body. I laid silent, ignoring my new nickname.

10

I began to visit Jack after work more regularly. I went
to his flat to prevent Maria asking him to come over to
ours for dinner yet again. I mean, four times in one week!
FOUR TIMES! I'd seen those eyes before, the same eyes
that caught my attention in '04. They were my eyes, not
his. I began to ask questions that at first festered then mul-
tiplied inside of my mind. Does comfort eventually wear
off? Does the challenge get too easy? Does she want
something more, someone else? I tormented myself daily
until bags of tired torture hung below my eyes. I had left
my car overnight in a multi-storey carpark so that Jack
and I could have a real bromance together. A couple of
rounds on the PlayStation; Domino's pizza, lots of lager
and maybe a cheeky ten bag just for old times' sake.
Neither of us were big on drugs but the odd smoke was
more nostalgic than it was addictive. I left work at five
and by the time I had told my colleagues what the Friday
night plan consisted of, locked all my shit away and got
out the door, it was nearly half past five. I rang Jack to ask
what he wanted on his pizza, I don't know why I
bothered. Every order since we were kids had always been
the same. "Margherita BRO!" he replied in a dickhead
way that I used to entertain. My pizza had a little more
spice, influenced of course by my wife Maria. Spicy
jalapeños, pepperoni, onions and a garlic stuffed crust. If
Clay was ordering, he would have gone full Texas BBQ
but Clay had surpassed us all these days. He had started
seeing someone. A work colleague by the name of
Christina. The two had grown quite fond of one and other, I was pleased. The pizzas were still warm by the time I
arrived at Jack's door. He greeted me the way he had always greeted his two compadres, with an opened bottle of

beer cool from the fridge. We traded gifts and that first gulp will forever be in my mind — the taste of something so fresh before the taste of something so stale will always be my claim to a physical oxymoron. Jack had always been the typical sporting moron, to put it politely. So why did I feel like the biggest fool of all? I tried to push all of my jealous stupidity out of my head and enjoy the evening that lay ahead. I attempted to gulp down the biggest mouthful of denial that I could manage. Maria was at home, seemingly content, allowing boys to be boys. She had just settled into a new novel. One about a fat old detective chasing some loony called Brady. She told me it was the first of a trilogy so I made a note of the other two titles so that I could scoop them up on my way home from work one day next week. It wasn't until our intermission between games that I really lost my appetite to finish the last three slices of my pizza. Jack had gone to the toilet and I had spotted something within his flat that haunted my mind, so much so that it still lingers today. A single item and a knife through my heart.

11

What is love?
>Baby don't hurt me.
>Don't hurt me.
>>No more.

12

Jack had snaked out to the toilet because dead men struggle to walk. I regarded him with intent. He looked different although he was exactly the same, the same as he'd always been. My psychological torment was changing faces and playing tricks too clever for me to comprehend. I programmed games for a living yet my brain seemed to be playing the biggest of games against itself.

13

Smoke slithered in grey waves and dispersed into the autumn air until there was only faint streaks with the stale scent of death trailing behind. Maria's Mayfair stick laid there at a forty-five degree angle burning away in an ashtray brought over from Greece. Her legs were curled up on our sofa, her book was half read as her eyes continued to scan the pages with deep anticipation. Would Hodges finally get his hands on Brady? For Maria this was a way of escaping the real world, sinking into fiction. Isn't that the case for most readers? Maria tweezed the end of her cigarette, dropped more ash into the tray and allowed the glare from artificial light to reflect off the butt. Light carried itself from the butt across the midnight air, reflecting a certain shade of lipstick almost invisibly off various surfaces. After a moment of contemplation from the evening's final chapter, Maria folded her book closed and inhaled a deep and concentrated cloud of smoke into her lungs, she felt its burn warm her chest and immediately replaced that feeling with an overwhelming sense of guilt.

14

I muttered vacantly to myself as I waited for Jack to return, "Forgive me father, for I will sin."

15

Maria's phone sounded one of many modern digital alerts. The sort of bleep that alerts its owner of a new incoming text message. As she slid the digital touch screen lock from one side to the other, she smiled at the message in front of her. Her feeling of guilt was instantaneously replaced. She replied promptly and sank back into her chair. Maria picked her book back up and opened the page she closed only moments ago. Feeling more awake than ever, she slid away from reality and into fiction once more ... .

16

A smoked, burnt-out cigarette lay surrounded by ash in its tray. The mouth-end painted in a certain shade of lip-stick that was undeniably unique to Maria did not exhibit grey waves of thin smoke anymore, the waves had ceased hours ago. Maria was asleep. She had gone from reality to fiction and ended up in a third world. A world of dreams where she would be haunted by memories. She saw her mother's fragile frame displaying a very colourless and sunken face. She saw her father's body floating in the ocean grasping a bottle. She saw a man on t—

17

Jack had been in the bathroom quite some time before he returned. The intermissions that followed weren't half as long. Each time he returned his attempts at humour got worse, "Jesus man, what's your bladder made out of … steel? I'm pissing every hour here! Hey, open up another bottle would ya bud? You not finishing those slices?" Jack had eaten all of his to soak up the booze. "Nah I'm good man, full up. Fancy a cheeky J instead?" I asked as I pinged off another set of bottle caps. "Cheers!" He celebrated, taking his drink. "Yeah … cheers Jack!" We clanged bottles. "Light one up then man, let's blaze!"

I spent the next half hour remembering how to make a college joint. I almost gave up but persisted. We smoked the next few hours away and as our speech became slower, our minds became entwined, we reminisced. We spoke of the past but we spoke of how life had turned out for all three of us. Jack expressed how lonely he was and how lucky I was. He was probably right but I didn't need reminding, certainly not from him. As the conversations slowed down further, I picked my spot. I was high alright but I could still function, I had to function. I knew I wouldn't be able to sleep, not with this on my mind — not for a very long time. After bottling it up for hours, I opened my carbonated can of frustration. I let go of my inner demons.

18

A smoked, burnt-out cigarette lay surrounded by ash in its tray. The mouth-end painted in a certain shade of lipstick that was undeniably unique to Maria did not exhibit grey waves of thin smoke anymore, the waves had ceased some time ago. A smoked, burnt-out cigarette lay surrounded by ash in its tray, in Jack's flat.

19

"Jack, buddy ..." holding the smoke stick up, "whose is this, you don't smoke?"

"Huh?" His eyes were occasionally rolling back into their sockets but I wasn't going to let him sleep, not tonight, not before I got my answer. "Jack! My man! You don't smoke, the occasional biff with me but that's it." "Wazit mata?" he murmured as he sat, spread out on his cheap sofa. "It matters to me. Whose is it?" I think the shock of my prodding sobered him up a little. Beginning to come round Jack looked up at me, I was standing over him holding the cigarette like a piece of evidence at a crime scene. To me, this was a crime scene. "Oh man, it was some girl's I was banging." Such a poor choice of words to come out with. "Oh yeah, who? When?" My questions were suddenly becoming more demanding, more urgent. Jack sat upright, ran his hands through his hair before deciding to speak through the gaps in his fingers, "Bro, I dunno. Some skank the other day. Who gives a shit right?"

"Don't you find it really fucking odd that the lipstick on this cigarette is the EXACT same lipstick Maria wears?" Jack's blank expression will forever haunt me because I didn't know if he was guilty or just scared. "Oh y ... yeah ... yeah sh—"

"What? WHAT?! WHAT?! JACK! Go on ... ."

"Maria did pop over the other day. Sh ... she wanted to t ... talk ideas for your birthday." His guilt was now overwhelming. It was as transparent as a sex worker's window in Amsterdam. "My birthday isn't for three fucking months! Besides, you just said it was from some 'skank' didn't you Jack?" Silence — a deafening, perpetual silence absorbed the room. I dropped Maria's cigarette onto Jack's floor and watched as my best friend's face struggled to show any emotion, any remorse. Then came the best form of defence, attack. "Get the fuck out man! NOW!"

"Don't worry pal, I'm leaving." Pal was not a word I had ever really used before. It seemed to fit perfectly into my exit, almost like it was scripted to end the scene.

Months passed and for the first time in my life I conquered a battle that I had been unable to conquer my entire life. In the months that followed, I dropped a tonne of weight. Although dropping that cigarette and seeing Jack's face as it hit his floor, made my heart feel a lot heavier than a tonne. The weight of my heart was eventually eased by the fact that Jack decided to move away. Without word or warning he just disappeared into the night along with his guilt and shame. We never spoke again and when both Maria and Clay asked the question, I explained that he had something to take care of, something personal and wasn't likely to be back anytime soon. Clay knew that Jack and I were the closer two out of our three-man group and Maria was presumably trying to hide her own guilt by not prodding me too hard for a deeper explanation on Jack. Had I ruined my closest and most historical friendship? Had I accused my best friend of betrayal based upon an inaccurate and psychologically exaggerated presumption? Had my own green demon finally pushed away the one person who just enjoyed my company? Or had Jack Toddinger been inside the only woman I had ever truly loved?

20

It was now mid-winter and the air had a frightfully bitter chill. Messages on Maria's phone added warmth to my cold hands by reigniting a fire that appeared to have died down months ago. I couldn't prove that Jack and Maria had snaked around behind my back, at least, that was my train of thought a few months back. I actually began to believe that Maria had popped round to sort out my birthday. Maria wasn't technically gifted and why would she need to be with someone like me around? She foolishly passed me her phone one afternoon to sort a glitch out within one of her apps and the devil inside me couldn't resist. The horned being that was stabbing away at my heart and chewing my brains had to look for answers — answers to a situation that may have never even existed. Maria passed me her phone and went into town for an hour or two, I think she felt free without it. It didn't stand out at first, kind of like Where's Wally (and I had been the Wally) so I had to look harder. I had to set aside denial to find the truth. There, buried under the name 'Jackie (Work)' was a thread of messages that revealed all I needed to know and all I didn't want to believe to be true. It was like a letter from the devil and the devil was Jack. Those frequent bathroom trips during our bromance made a lot more sense. They made an opportunity for him to message my not so innocent wife. I closed down all the apps and restarted her phone, the glitch cleared itself. On this island, Maria seemed to be slow at just the basics. I waited for her to return. She skipped through the door, unaware of what I had found. I passed her device of deceit back and received a kiss, the sort of kiss you'd have given your grandma when she gave you your birthday card that held a note inside of it. We carried on our day and all I could think about was the messages I had glanced over, I restudied them in my mind's eye to make sure there couldn't be any doubt. Then, something sinister sprung to mind. Had Maria been with Clay as well? None of us had ever seen this

Christina and nothing from the people around me would surprise me now. My head began to conjure so many demons inside even darker scenarios that I no longer knew what was real.

21

Goodbye.

22

I was alone at home the following day. I had taken the day off from work without notifying the woman that wore a wedding ring and slept in my bed. I didn't need a plan because I knew exactly how I wanted this to play out. My gaunt face began to show splinters of bone pushing through under skin, stress-related diets were underrated. Winter found it easier to penetrate and shake my bones because I had no meat to insulate them. I sat there all day in my kitchen, alone. Thinking of who I'd miss and who'd miss me. Between both concepts I couldn't think of a single name. The light of day dimmed itself around me and painted a faint silhouette on the wall behind me. This evening would be my last one here, my last one ever. The kitchen clock turned its arms to display six in the evening. I had been sat there all day, just thinking and thinking and thinking. Any moment now … .

23

Maria had finished her day and walked the longer

route home past Jack's. She knew he had disappeared off the grid because she hadn't heard from him since I said he was leaving — no call and no text. She looked up at his flat and squinted in puzzlement at his abrupt disappearing act. Was he just teasing her? Did he want her to start the chase, to up sticks and get away from it all? She bit her lip at the possibility and carried on home to her husband, to me. One last stop at the local off-licence to pick up some essentials, namely a bottle of wine for dinner. The perfect wife.

24

As the door lock turned and sprung open Maria was greeted by an eerie darkness, a still darkness that carried the thoughts of my mind in the air. She must have presumed that I had stopped on after work, squashing bugs. Maria sung to herself to ease the tension of darkness before she put the kitchen lights on. She placed the bottle of wine on the worktop and put the five pence carrier bag of groceries on the table. The stairs took her up to the bedroom where she planned to undress and shower ready for my arrival. Walking into the bedroom she simultaneously pulled the blinds shut. Feeling more comfortable that she wasn't putting on an exhibition she slid down her clothes and stood there in only her bra and thong, admiring her slim physique in our bedroom mirror. Her white lingerie complimented her olive skin as the two contrasted against one and other underneath false lighting. She smiled back at herself in the mirror, pleased she hadn't aged badly and just as she was about to slide her thong down past her knees, I stepped out to greet my darling wife.

"FU … FUCK!" Maria screamed as she pulled her fingers out from the laced waistband. A momentary pause revealed who was in the room with her. She began to giggle ever so gently in relief — familiarity is a face that welcomes you home. "W ... what the hell are you doing baby? You scared me!" Her brows furrowed. "Why the hell are you hiding behind the door like that?" Her relief morphed into concerned confusion. "I was watching you." I said ever so calmly, almost emotionless.

"Haha, you don't need to spy on me if you want to see me undress baby." Once a tease, always a tease. Her flirtatious ways now seemed to repulse me. "I wasn't spying. I was observing." I said with slight venom.

"Yeah yeah, same thing perv. How come you're a little freaky tonight and what's that you're holding?" Her two questions were said in quick succession, undercoated with slight panic so that they merged into one. So I merged my answers, "Let me show you baby." I walked forward, towards her. "I'll be your last." I said with dead emotion only someone with my current mindset could really understand. "W ... WHA—" and before she could question me further, I struck her with a medium-sized rusty hammer that I had gripped tightly in my right hand. Maria fell back hard and fast, the way we had once fallen for each other all those years ago.

25

Half conscious with blood dripping down the front of her forehead, I often wonder how much Maria felt of me sliding in and out of her. Vicious thrusts made me feel powerful. She was helpless and so desperate for air that the abuse was almost a secondary concern. She gasped like a goldfish out of water and I kept attacking like a shark in blood. She nearly sat up once but as I beat her back down with my fist, she surrendered almost instantaneously. The life in her body was growing limp by the second, I loved it. I carried on the abuse throughout the night, I didn't want it to end. I kept her just conscious enough to make sure she suffered. There was a moment, a moment when I caught my own reflection staring back at me in the mirror. The rush that I got watching myself on Maria was so powerful, so perfect, so justified. He had a pokey face. The kind that looked like it had more bone than skin. The kind that looked like it was caving in on itself. His jawline was prominent and his eyes were beady — beady like the rain that slid down the glass of our bedroom window. Especially during that winter's evening.

26

After I could go no more I beat my wife with the rusty hammer until her skull was so misshaped, it resembled a punctured football. I think I eventually repainted over the rust in a lovely cardinal. Hammering down on her body instead of inside it was like watching Maria dance — dance at my cardinal carnival.

27

I remember nothing directly after the thrill of it all. Apparently I was standing over her butchered body, naked and dripping in DNA. I think I remember still being hard when the cold from metal handcuffs clamped around my wrists. I was clenching the repainted hammer so tightly in my right hand that it took two police officers to prise it from me. I vaguely remember an empty bottle of Rioja on the bed and remnants of a shot glass around the room. The shards of glass smelt like they had travelled. Just out of sight in the corner of the room was another bottle. This one was unlabelled and only half-empty. A small stain had formed on the carpet around the neck where some of its contents had oozed out. The clear liquid that sat in and around the bottle had the same distinctive scent as the shards around the room, both smelt of Greece. The police later told me that I called them, that I reported it all. I remember nothing directly after the thrill. I now sit here in cell B2 as a prisoner within a category A prison. I have a number that serves as identification. To my inmates I'm 'The Paperboy' because all I have been doing since they locked me up in B2, is writing all of this down. Maybe I write to remember, maybe it's to forget. I have no real idea why I write at all anymore but I cannot shake that reflection … that reflection. His eyes were grey. Piercingly grey. They glinted in every direction but they seemed to glint just that little bit more when they stared back at me.

He had a pokey face — the man that raped and murdered my wife … especially during that winter's evening.

ACKNOWLEDGEMENTS

After spending around a decade of doing anything *but* writing, I finally stopped texting and started typing. Writing a story is one of the most mentally challenging (and exhausting) things I have ever done! At the same time, when that final sentence falls onto the page, there's a sense of accomplishment I will forever struggle to explain.

There's a list of people that have not only motivated me but also helped me to organise the words that have bounced around inside of my head. Without you, my chapters would still be just a mad man's thoughts.

I'd like to start by thanking my English teachers who took an interest in my writing from an early age. The confidence that you both injected into me taunted and haunted me for a decade thereafter. I battled with myself as to whether I could actually do it — as to whether I could actually write a story. I hope I didn't let you down.

What's a man without his woman? A massive thank you (and kiss) goes out to my queen. She hears the ideas, reads the drafts and is honest enough to tell me when either one is not at the level they need to be. I always aim to amaze you, because you amaze me.

Finally, I'd like to thank all the people that read any drafts that I sent to them and who listened to me babble on about various plots and ideas. Your feedback is more powerful than any story I write because they give final versions more life than their drafts.

To anybody I forgot to mention, I've left the space below for you to write your name down.

ABOUT THE AUTHOR

Luke Settle

Luke Settle is a British fiction author in his early thirties. His debut thriller, the short story *A Certain Shade of Lipstick* is his first public release. Luke has spent over a decade writing and producing music but decided to go on hiatus in order to embrace his passion in literature. He currently resides in rural Lincolnshire with his partner Carly and their pet 'dinosaur' Rex.

Printed in Great Britain
by Amazon

22715639R00020